Written by Harriet Ziefert

Lunchtime for a Purple Snake

Paintings by Todd McKie

HOUGHTON MIFFLIN COMPANY, BOSTON 2003

Walter Lorraine ⊛ Books

For Will, who's a great painting partner
—H.Z.

For Jesseca, Judy, and Jesse
—T.M.

Walter Lorraine (wl) Books

Text copyright © 2003 by Harriet Ziefert
Illustrations copyright © 2003 by Todd McKie
All rights reserved. For information about permission
to reproduce selections from this book, write to
Permissions, Houghton Mifflin Company,
215 Park Avenue South, New York, New York 10003.

www.houghtonmifflinbooks.com

Library of Congress Cataloging-in-Publication Data

Ziefert, Harriet.
Lunchtime for a purple snake / by Harriet Ziefert ;
illustrated by Todd McKie.
p. cm.
Summary: When Jessica visits her artist grandpa
they make a painting together.
ISBN 0-618-31133-5
[1. Grandfathers—Fiction. 2. Artists—Fiction. 3. Color—Fiction.]
I. McKie, Todd, 1944- ill. II. Title.
PZ7.Z487 Lu 2003
[E]—dc21
2002010295

Printed in China for Harriet Ziefert, Inc.
1 3 5 7 9 10 8 6 4 2

My name is Jessica. When I'm big,
I want to be an artist, just like my grandpa.

I love to visit my grandpa's studio.

When I go there, we paint together.

Grandpa cleans off his drawing table.
Then he puts a big piece of paper in the middle.
Grandpa fills the water pots. He cleans a palette
and squeezes five colors of paint—red, yellow,
blue, black, and white.

I want more colors, but Grandpa says,
"Five are enough to make all the colors
of the rainbow."

Grandpa teaches me to mix colors. Do you know that a little red and a little blue make **PURPLE**?

A little red and a little yellow make **ORANGE**.

A little blue and a little yellow make **GREEN**.

Black makes a color darker. But you have to add black slowly. If you add too much, it makes the paint the color of MUD!

White makes a color lighter. "Look! a dab of red and a dot of white—mix them together and you have PINK."

Sometimes I put too much paint on the brush.
It drips and I make a big blob. I get mad.

Grandpa says, "It's all right, Jessica. All artists make mistakes. And sometimes you can turn a mistake into something good."

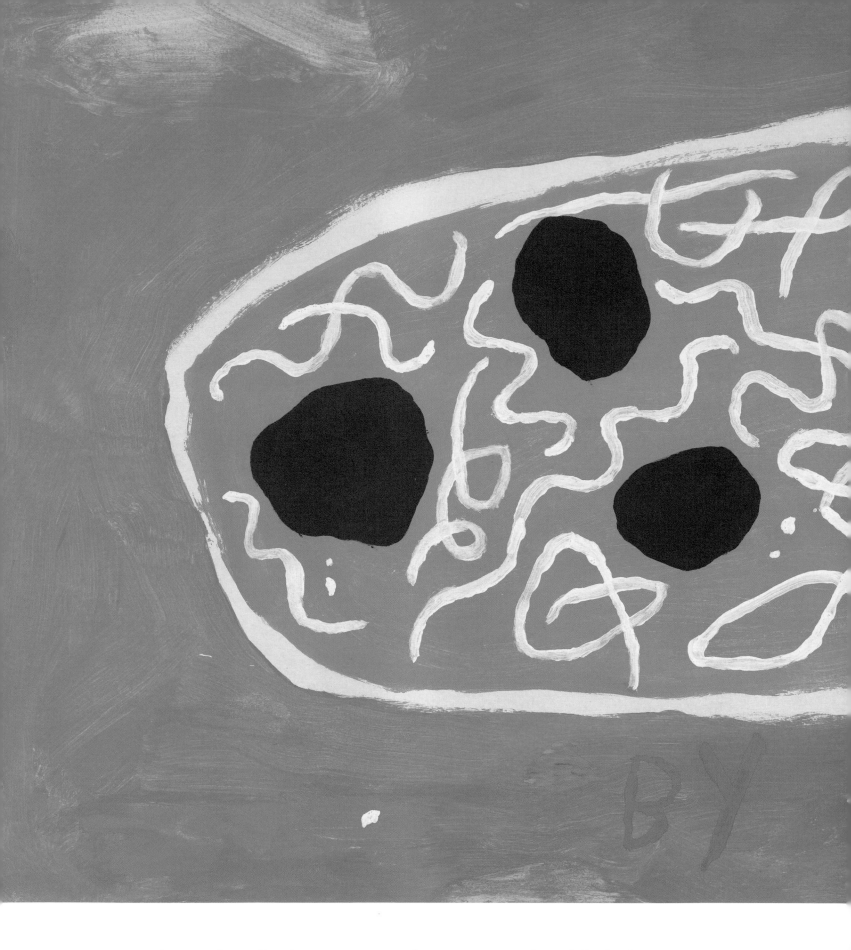

Grandpa helps me and we turn the blob into
meatballs and spaghetti. I want to add a little
Parmesan cheese, but Grandpa warns me that if

I keep on painting, the picture will "go dead." I'm not exactly sure what Grandpa means, but I'm willing to believe him. I say, "Okay, no cheese. I'm done!"

Grandpa likes to listen to music while he works, so he turns on jazz music. Then he unrolls a clean piece of paper. He says,

"Don't start right away. Take time to choose your colors. Try to make the paint sing."

"Okay, Grandpa. I'll try to make the colors sing."

I start on one side of the big piece of paper.
"What are you making?" Grandpa asks.

I answer that I'm making a slithery snake.

"Then I'll make a bug for him to eat," says Grandpa.
"I'll give it six green legs and some light green
stripes on its back."

While Grandpa paints the bug, I clean my brush.
When he's done, I dip my brush into black and say,
"Now I'll make a rock for the snake to slither on."

"And I'll make a flower for him to look at,"
Grandpa says. "A great big flower with orange
petals and a blue center."

I watch Grandpa carefully paint tiny dots in the center of the flower, then I say, "I'll make a sun to keep the snake warm while he's catching bugs."

And so we paint.

Fluffy clouds . . . nice green grass . . . pretty plants . . .

and two blue birds . . .

until our picture is finished.

Then Grandpa puts the painting on a line
so it can dry . . . just like laundry!

He asks me for a title. I think a little,
then I give my answer:

Lunchtime for a Purple Snake